WITHDRAWN

D1170745

# When Fish and Bird Meet

Written by Chunhua Huang
Illustrated by Manon Gauthier

When Fish sees Bird,
she joyfully blows
bubbles.

When Bird sees Fish,
he cheerfully chirps.

"Why not come UP here?" asks Bird.

"Why not come **down** here?" asks **Fish.**

"Look! I can **fly**."

"Look! I can **swim**."

"I can **fly** over the **trees.**"

"I can go down deep to the bottom of the sea."

"I can **fly**
**up high**
in the **sky**."

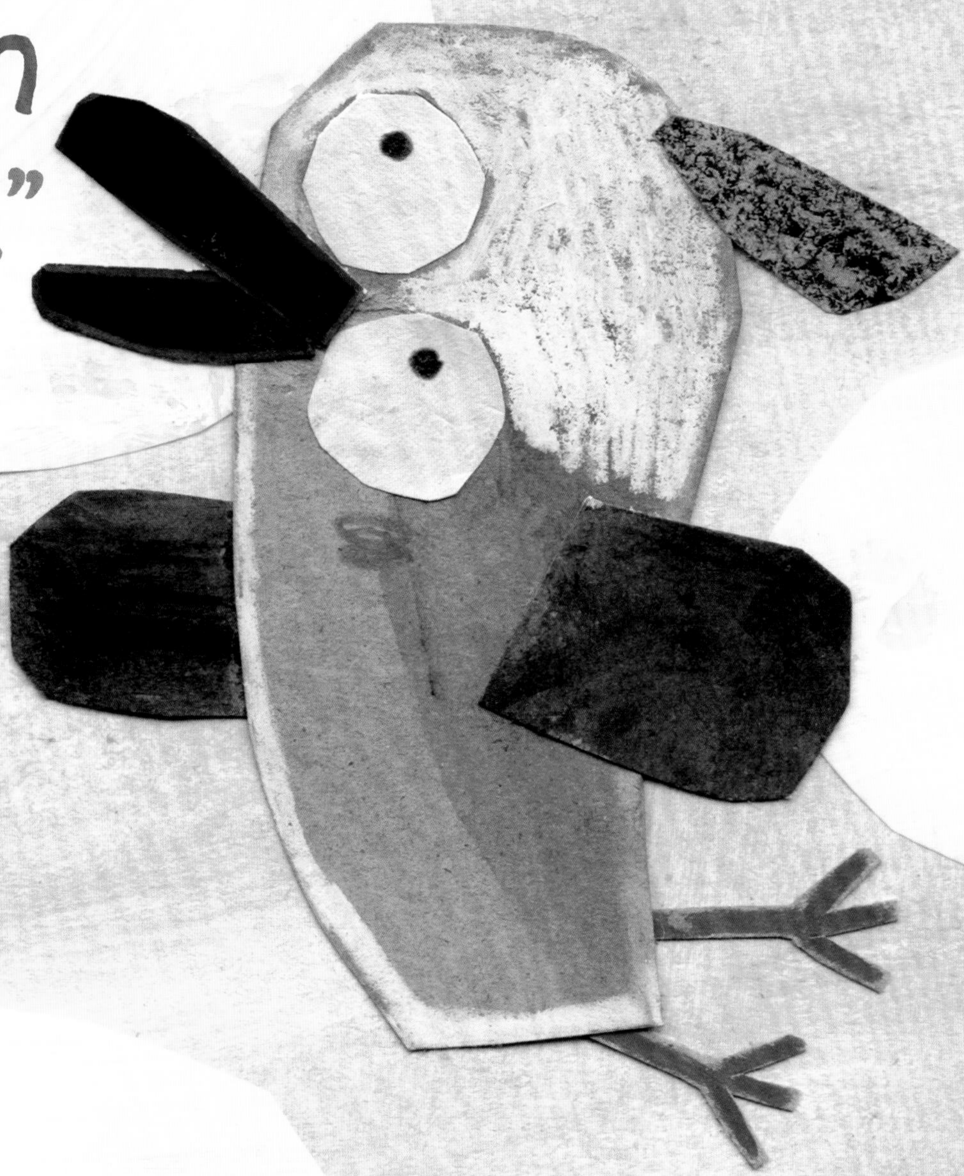

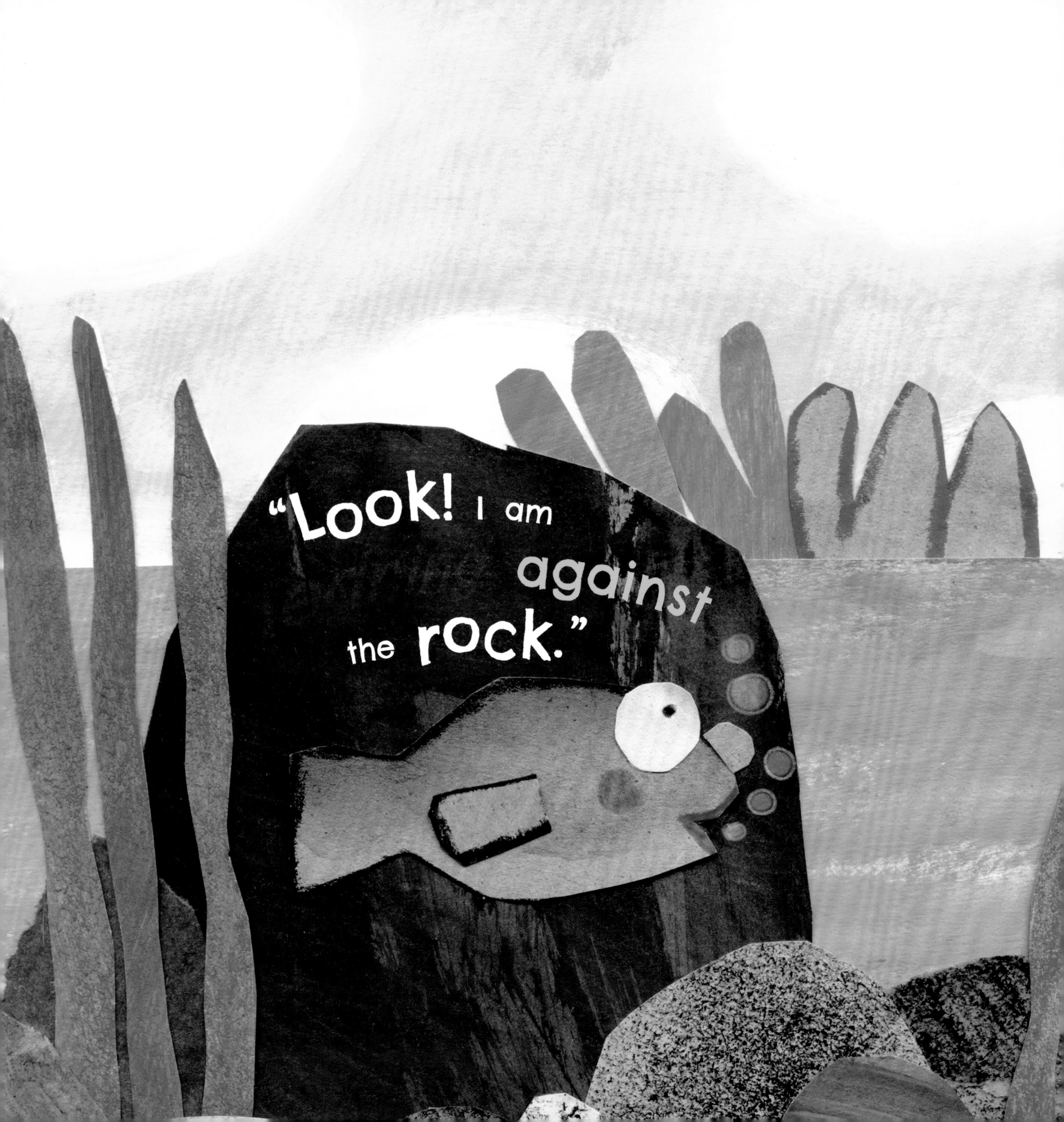

"Look! I am against the rock."

"Look! I am perching on the rock."

"I'll tell you the story of how I **caught** the **shrimp**."

"I'll tell you the story of how I pecked the worm."

"Let's meet again soon!"

# Chunhua Huang

 is a member of the Chinese Writers' Association and vice chairman of the Wuhan Writers' Association. His works have won the Bingxin Children's Literature New Writing Award and the Children's Literature Magazine Annual Award.

# Manon Gauthier

 is a well-known Canadian children's book illustrator. Her books have been translated into many languages. She is especially skilled at creating stories using collage.